VICTORIA

THE RISE OF A QUEEN

Book Dedication

I dedicate this book to the memory of my Dad,
His meals for friends and family,
were the best I ever had.

And to my Godly Mom,
for the example you are,
Your support through the years
has helped me go far.

Then to my loving husband,
who is always so reliable,
A man of God, whose kind heart and loving words
are always undeniable.

To all my family and friends,
for your faith and love,
Thanks for your support,
may you be blessed from God above.

TABLE OF CONTENTS

INTRODUCTION

My name is Queen Victoria, Queen of the Seven Kingdoms (second-in-command).

Before I was Queen, I was just an angel enjoying life in the cosmos and learning about all the different kingdoms; nothing was required of me, but to enjoy my freedom. It was a simple life, an easy life, one that many would love. Yet, after all I have been through, I would not go back there for the entire world.

I had peace. I had safety. I had time. I was a free spirit being that enjoyed a life without challenges.

All that changed three thousand years ago. What a journey it has been since then. My, my, I can hardly believe that I am telling this story! I will understand if you do not believe me, but I promise that every word is true. A Queen does not lie to her people, and if you're reading this, you are one of mine.

That is a matter for another time, though.

For now, I want to introduce you to my world.

Hmm, where do I begin? Well, I was born in a place called the Darkness of Stars; a place where no light shines. This place cannot be found by anyone, but the King and his sons.

I was three years old, human age, when I was released from that place.

I serve the King. He has no beginning or end, he has no mother or father, he is the creator of us all. He is a King of order and duties. He rules over all.

Before I was born, he created three heavens: The first heaven is the earth's atmosphere, the second heaven is where the moon, sun, stars, and the planets reside, and the third heaven is the heaven of heavens where I live with my king.

I was raised to understand his ways, the ways he created. Our laws are the old laws, covered by heroism and honor. We follow codes set by the old order, which began with the King. Our politics may seem strange to the people of the earth Kingdom, but these rules are in place to keep order.

All the heavens operate in rank and in order by laws that humankind must learn and master. They have lost their way; tainted by their own importance. Too many angels have fallen for the same reason.

In the third heaven, where I dwell, we work as well in rank and in order. For example, we have three sections of angelic beings with three unique kinds of angelic beings within each section. We are spirit beings with no physical body, but we can take on the appearance of mankind to communicate with humans. We even walk around in heaven, sometimes in human form. The first section comprises those who adore the King directly, the second section contains the ones who fulfill the King's plan on the earth, and third section holds the ones that interact and serve mankind; I was in this section but didn't know things were about to shift.

However, in this section there are: Principalities, Archangels, and Angels; I was an angel. As an angel, we praise our King, fight against evil, deliver messages to mankind, and ministering to mankind.

Although it was easy with our astral power, I loved what I did. I was on the battlefield. At this time, being eighty-nine, I have seen and done so much.

When I was much younger in age, I was a happy spirit; always staying close to my mentors and brothers (Gabriel, Michael, and Raphael). Believe it or not, we start operating as soon as we are born, because our king's purpose and mission is of great importance. I remember a few things as a young angel, which is valid to my story that I must share for you to understand.

This story has been repeated in our Kingdom many times, but it has not been told in yours.

Chapter 1

My name is Victoria. I was raised in the deepest parts of the heavens where true light shines. I grew up here under the supervision of the King and my older brothers. In the astral sphere we do not care about gender roles in leadership.

My role was chosen because destiny selected me. I am both the youngest and the last child of my line. This means that it is my duty to raise the Next Generation. I am the star that will light the sky and join all. Let me introduce you to my brothers.

Gabriel, my older brother, bears messages from the heavens to earth. He is kind, strong, and powerful. Our brothers Michael and Raphael are jokesters. The other angels think they are so serious, but in secret, they are funny and cheerful. They teach me knowledge, wisdom, understanding, and love: all that is needed to stay pure in the world. I have been told it's very hard to be pure in the world of Mankind. They say that one day, I will understand why I am being taught all these things and why it's imperative to lead with the King of Heaven's will. Being that I live in Heaven, I'm not sure why I need to learn the skills of Earth.

As time goes on, I ask my brothers why Gabriel is always so busy and never has time to spend with us.

"A time will come when others close to you will ask the same question," replies Michael.

I say, "Michael, I never understand you."

He shrugs. "One day, you will."

As I get older, stronger, and wiser, I get to see more of my older brother and spend time with him. I have always wondered about our parents. My brothers never speak about our parents, but Raphael says that I have my mother's eyes and smile.

When we were younger, they used to play tag with me around the heavens. Once, I found my way into a garden, it was beautiful and bountiful. Fresh fruit hung all over and there was a snake. He was slender, scaly, and shined like a jewel. When Raphael found me, I thought he was angry that I had found such a good hiding place, which was not the case. He told me that I was too important to be lost and that we could not play again. How little did I know what he meant.

I must say, the heavens are beautiful, breathtaking, and divine. I love standing on the rooftop of my fortress while gazing out at all that surrounds me.

I hear the melody of both joy and sadness. I can feel it. Something is coming!

I hear a female voice say, "My daughter, you're so beautiful. I can see the power within you. Get ready because, after tonight, your eyes will be open to what is known and unknown to others."

Frightened by the strange voice, I yell, "Who are you, and why do you call me your daughter? My parents are dead!"

There was no reply. I could not stop thinking about the voice.

All night, I ponder on the words of this strange voice, and I keep asking myself about what was going to happen to me as she had predicted. I get up the next day, get dressed, and walk down the stairs only to see Gabriel standing at the bottom of the staircase with a scroll in his hand.

He says with a stern voice, "Victoria, follow me."

He guides me to a hidden wall I pass by every day. On the other side of this wall is a dark and narrow hallway I can see right through with stars I have never seen before. Immense power and strength are thrumming through them. We walk through another secret wall where the beauty of the room is indescribable. There, I see Michael and Raphael, who are holding scrolls. Gabriel takes me to an ancient chair covered with markings in the old language of the King and tells me to sit. One of the symbols on the chair is a crown with a thunderbolt going around it as if it were one with the crown.

While my three brothers stand in front of me, shoulder-to-shoulder, Gabriel speaks, "Listen, Victoria, this is your assignment from the King himself…

Victoria—Angel and Princess of the Northern Kingdom, you will soon wear the crown of the seven kingdoms in which lie all our secrets. Starting tomorrow, you will be tested to see if you are fit to become the ruler over each kingdom."

Up until this moment, my brothers had never introduced me to the book of prophecy. How was I supposed to know all this? It was a tremendous amount of information to process in such a short time.

I stop my brother and ask, "What do you mean by 'ruler over the seven kingdoms'?"

"Victoria, one day, you will have to take your place as the rest of us. To take your rightful place, you must meet the necessary qualifications. It's time for you to be tested and apply the wisdom that you have acquired over the years."

I didn't understand what he was saying. I frowned while asking, "But brother, I am still learning and growing. I'm not even a hundred years old yet!"

Gabriel says, "As your older brother, I command you to be silent and listen!

Gabriel continued, "Victoria, each of the seven kingdoms serves as a partial gift that you must contain within your heart before becoming the ruler of these magnificent worlds. You must understand and govern following the laws of each kingdom. Do not be deceived by the tricks. Your brothers and I will take turns in guiding you through the test, but we will not assist you. We will show you to the doors, but only you can enter. You will receive three gifts, but you can only use one of these gifts at a time while being tested. As per the stars, you have lived almost ten decades, and the time is now to take your place in the kingdom prepared for you to rule."

They didn't bother explaining much to me, but this was because I was the youngest. I am nervous.

What could be coming next!

CHAPTER 2

I stay very still. It is unusual for my brothers to give me such a firm order, so I know that this is very important.

This isn't one of their tricks or jokes. Each one of them is holding a scroll. Everything in Heaven is written because we understand the power of the word. Mankind has also started to understand the power of spoken words.

Michael reads from his scroll, "Victoria, these tasks will not only strengthen you but also make you the most powerful Queen ever. There has only been one Queen of the seven kingdoms before you. She was beautiful and wise, but she lacked understanding of some matters. If you complete the tests of the seven kingdoms, I am commanded by the King to tell you everything about this Queen who failed the humans." I knew that there was a Queen once, but nobody would speak to me about it. I know that they have been planning it for decades by the formality of the whole thing. I sit and listen as I have been instructed, trying to take in everything that they say.

Raphael reads from his scroll, "Victoria, if you complete the test of the seven kingdoms and accept your position as Queen, I will present you with a gift from the King himself."

As I sit and listen to them read each scroll, I wonder why the King chose a daughter with no parents, who is being raised by her siblings. After the scrolls were read, my brothers look at me and ask if I am ready.

I do not know if I am ready! I do not know what I am taking on. There must have been a reason why he chose me, but it had never occurred to me; it might have to do with destiny. I must take on this quest and become the ruler of the seven kingdoms. I just don't know what that entails yet.

Raphael says, "Are you ready?"

I reply, "Yes, but only if I can speak to the King."

Gabriel laughs and says, "The King told me you would ask that. My brothers say you will see the King tomorrow, Victoria."

Waiting is difficult for me. I have so many questions.

Why me?

Why now?

Why not one of my brothers?

Could he not have chosen the youngest brother?

They had so much more experienced than me. Everything I have learned; I have learned from them. They have taught me so much. Why am I so special? I do not want to fall asleep, but I do.

I have a dream, a dream of a pretty woman with eyes just like mine who extend a hand to me and raises my chin to look at her.

She tells me, "You are finally ready", but before I can ask anything else it is morning.

The following day comes, and I wake up excited. As I walk down the stairs, I see two of my brothers waiting for me; as usual, Gabriel is on an assignment from the King.

Michael says, "Let's go over a few rules. When you walk into the throne room, cover your eyes with your wings and bow down. Before you speak, the King must acknowledge you."

Order and hierarchy are important to angels. We believe very much in respect and there is no one I respect more than the King. My brother does not need to remind me to be polite. Unlike him, I am always polite, especially when it comes to the King. I know exactly how to show him respect. I have been a good student and I have learned well. Admittedly though, I have never been in the throne room before. A shiver of excitement runs across my wings, making every tiny line on my feathers flutter.

I arrive in the throne room. It's filled with love, beauty, and angels. I have never seen anything this beautiful before. I bow down as instructed and cover my eyes with my wings.

I hear a strong, masculine voice saying, "Victoria, my child, I give you some of my power."

He touches my chest and mind, and suddenly something in me breaks. I feel free, powerful, and all-knowing. This was not what I was expecting, and I faint. I fall to the floor in a puddle of feathers, but nobody catches me. Someone could have warned me! I suspect that my brothers meant to but for their own amusement did not tell me. I will get them back for that. I can feel my body floating into space in the emptiness of the dark.

And then, there is nothing.

I wake up in my room. As I lie in bed, I wonder what happened. I walk over to the mirror and look at my wings. They have gotten bigger and stronger! My heart and mind feel free; it's hard to explain. It is something I cannot put into words, but it was almost what you humans would call a light switch moment. Something has changed in me, for the better.

I hear Raphael calling for me, "Victoria, come on, it's time. It's time for your first test."

I am barely awake from my slumber and still having difficulty processing all of this. I wonder, "what's the rush?' After all, given the fact that we live for hundreds of years, why are they so insistent on rushing? In hindsight, I was so naïve, as every second counts. More so, then I could ever understand at the time.

I ask, "What test? What happened to me? How did I end up here in my bed? Someone please explains to me what happened."

I hear Raphael walking upstairs to my room.

He slowly opens the door and says, "Come with me to a private area where no one can hear us talk."

I follow him down the hall to the bridge room.

After we walk into the bridge room, he closes the door and says, "Let the darkness engulf the room; in darkness and emptiness we stand."

The room turns into an empty, dark space where no one is around. It is pure darkness. There is not even a single start to give a faint outline of his body. I can see nothing. The black is completely engulfing. Even without being able to see, I can tell by the sound of his voice that we must act quickly.

"Victoria, I'm not supposed to tell you this, but the King can't waste time or energy; he anointed you with some of his power. This power makes you stronger and more intelligent, and you can see weaknesses. After you finish your first and second test, I will sit you down in an emptied space like this where it's just you and me. No one can access the realm. I will then tell you a story that was purposely hidden from certain angels in the kingdom and the rest of humans. It will explain why you are being tested before you take your place. It will explain why the King anointed you before your test begins. The main reason is to explain the unknown voice you heard."

I look at my brother and say, "Please, tell me the whole story with every detail because if I am supposed to be Queen, I need to know every detail."

He agrees, but before he can say anything else, the darkness turns to light, and we are back at home.

I do not get my answers, but they will appear in the days to come. There is no turning back. I know I am strong. I know I can do it. Even without preparation, there is a small glimmer in my insides that tells me that this is what I am supposed to do. I have finally found the path towards my destiny.

Everyone in this world has a destiny that they must fulfill. It is important to seek it out. You may not know what it is, or even that you have one, but when the time comes you will know. When you place your foot down on the path of your destiny, you will sense the moment I speak of is before you. The feelings and emotions that flood throughout the body are different for everyone, but I can guarantee you will know. I know, and I will claim it along my own road.

It is time for my first test, and who better to pass with flying colors than an angel with such ginormous wings?

CHAPTER 3

Wings beating against the soft air around me as I try to leave my thoughts behind. As I concentrate on the excited energy that is pulsing through my veins. It starts to dawn on me how important all of this must be. There is no room for mistake and no room for error. I give a nervous swallow.

Whether or not I want to do this is no longer a question. Every bone in my body is saying yes, yes, yes. I feel as though I may be ready, but although I am confident, I am not stupid enough to feel arrogance. There is a part of me that worries.

What will this test be?

What will I have to do?

Will I be able to accomplish it?

How long will it take?

What happens if I fail?

There is only one way to find out!

Raphael says, "Your first test will be on wisdom. Wisdom is to recognize the right course of action and to have the heart and courage to follow it.

"There are two worlds. One world is full of darkness and sin, and the other world is full of light and peace. Do you make the decision to keep them separated, or do you slowly introduce more light into the darkness without corrupting the light? Before you answer, ponder on it and ask yourself some questions such as why the world is so dark. The test may seem simple, but it's really not, Victoria."

I am glad that this is a test of the mind. I have been raised to be knowledgeable and considerate. It is left to me to decide. As an angel free will is not something which I often need to consider, but as I am given the choice I think hard. I never thought about this part of being a leader. I am used to following the rules, but as times change a leader must be able to set them. It seems silly, but I have not considered this before. The amount of power that is within my hands seems almost... Dangerous? I do not want to make the wrong decision. My King is trusting me. I can do this.

I walk out to watch the stars and to observe the darkness hovering over the earth from heaven's window. I can see the love and peace fading. I also see the lifespan on Earth being shortened because of sin. There is not much light, but the part of the world that is reflecting light shines brightly.

"How can you introduce more light to a world that is mostly full of darkness?" she asked herself.

"Victoria, what is your answer?"

I feel like I have not had long enough to think. I do not need to think however, this is a decision but should be made with my heart. Or at least I think it is. I am about to find out, so I give my answer.

"I will incorporate more light into the world with a single touch of love but not as the world of corruption expects it."

Raphael looks at me and says, "'You are still lacking wisdom."

"I don't understand."

He replies, "You will understand as soon as the star draws closer, and, Victoria, your answer has no explanation; you must explain how. Come with me. Let me show you the world of corruption."

I feel like I have failed, but he has not told me so. He must be giving me the opportunity to extend my answer. Does that mean I am on the right track? My heart said so, so it must be true.

He takes me in for a closer look and I am reminded of that childhood day with the snake. The same intoxicating fascination comes over me. It was only after that I realized that I had been saved from something quite dark. From the heavens the Earth is a beautiful blue and a verdant green. This is the problem with getting the bigger picture. The small details matter. These are the fragments which build the entire thing. Details are the foundations of the greater structure. A house can look sturdy enough but if attention has not been paid to the details of the foundation it may soon crumble.

I take my first step into the other kingdom.

As I step onto Earth, darkness covers the whole land. I see people with evil spirits, not just one but many from previous generations. They're wearing them down. They are slaves to their own ancestors' wickedness. People are dying because of things they are not letting go. The sun is turning to blood, and people are suffocating because there is no oxygen, no sun, no peace, no love, and no understanding. The leadership is corrupt and cannot even see the darkness they carry within them.

"Victoria, explain to me how you are going to incorporate love into the darkness."

He is not blessed with the eyes of the Chosen and I gain confidence.

I look at my brother and say, "It can be done."

He seemed impressed at my determined answer, but he does not tell me it is correct.

Raphael and I go back home, and he says, "Tomorrow there will be another test, so be prepared. Oh, and don't think you have passed this test. You must still ponder on this one while preparing for tomorrow's test. After tomorrow's test we will sit down and discuss your answers. The King will inform you if you passed or failed. However, you still get to finish answering test one before completing test two."

As I go upstairs, I hear the same voice again, and this time, she says, "Daughter, you need more than love to change the darkness. Where is your strategy and where is your understanding and knowledge?"

"Who are you?" I say. "Why are you helping me?"

The voice replies, "Ask Gabriel."

Why can I not have a straight answer?

I sigh heavily.

"I suppose I must talk to Gabriel then, but what does it all mean?"

I know that my King would not put me on a false track. I have full faith in him. It does not stop it from being frustrating though!

The part of me that had awaken to feel powerful started to light up other areas of me. One is a yearning to do right by humans. I wish to be able to rule over them and help them in all their endeavors, but first I must pass these tests. Now I understand why every second counts. Not to mention the fact that human lives are so much shorter than our own.

CHAPTER 4

I hear Gabriel coming upstairs.

He says, "Victoria, are you alright?"

I reply, "No. I heard a female voice that is telling me I need to have a strategy. When I asked her who she was, she said to ask Gabriel. Who is this woman? What is going on, brother?"

He looks at me with inexplicable anger in his eyes. There is almost a flame flickering within them. I have never seen him look at anyone, be that angel, man or spirit, in such a way. To say the least, it is a little frightening, but what else was I supposed to do?

To ask questions is to learn. Seeking knowledge seeks a better life. It gives understanding which leads to better decisions. It isn't like my brothers have been very forthcoming with me anyway. I know that in the dark room the other day they overstretched a little and I am grateful for this, but I am left feeling like a leaf floating along the tide without knowing my way.

"Victoria, listen to me. Whatever you do, do not trust this person or go anywhere with this woman."

How can I go near her? She is no more than a disembodied voice to me? It does seem incredibly worrisome to him though. The tiny feathers on the tip of my quills stand at attention. I think in human terms it is called goosebumps, but up here we do not have such a thing. That is a symptom of something else—and let me mention there's is no such thing as illness or disease in that Kingdom. Therefore, our bodies do not need to give us warning signs. I cannot help but emotionally react though. I must know more!

"Brother, you still didn't tell me who she is."

"Don't worry. All you need to know is not to trust her."

I hear Gabriel calling my brothers, not like on Earth, but with his wings. See, our wings were made by the King's hands. He used dusk and feathers from the hidden realm, which he alone can enter. Now, the energy coming from the wings is so strong that even I start to feel an unknown frequency as if they were communicating in another realm.

Raphael and Michael appear from around the corner. It looks like they just came from battle. They immediately know it is urgent and go into a room I have never seen before. It is very old and ancient. I realize that my brothers have lots of secrets: secret rooms, realms, and unknown tales of horror. I can tell that this room was hidden from me for a reason. I thought I knew every part of this fortress, but apparently not. I use my secret necklace to hide from my brothers, so I can listen in on their conversation. Eavesdropping is most definitely a sin, but it is not a greater sin but letting bad things happen by not gathering information.

I am not of my brother's rank, not yet anyway. In our systems that means a lot. I should not be listening. Or should I? How do I know what is a part of these tests anymore?

And what my brother's say, I very much need to know.

I quietly crouch down, holding my necklace tightly so as not to be caught. It was a gift from Mother, not that I ever knew her or remember her. For this reason, as well as many others, I tried to keep it on me at all times. I fear if my brothers knew, or even the King, it might be taken away from me. Apart from my eyes and smile, it is the only thing I have opposed: my only physical possession.

Gabriel starts to talk, "Michael, she is back, and she is after Victoria. She is giving her advice and trying to get Victoria to trust her. Victoria will become Queen and defeat the old Queen. She has no right to be here. I know her innermost secrets and thoughts, and they are not good for the kingdom."

Michael says, "Gabriel, she is restricted from this realm. She has no power or authority here. Have you informed the King?"

That explains why I have not seen her in person then. She cannot enter. I wonder how her voice managed to get through. The defensive here are great and looking at my brother's rage they had no idea about anything going on until I mentioned it.

Gabriel replies, "No, I have not, but I am sure he already knows."

Raphael adds, "Grab my hand, and let's inform the King of his daughter."

There is a secret passage to the throne room, and I make it there just in time. The moment it shuts, they are there, and I do my best not to let them know but I am frazzled.

They have not noticed. Thankfully.

Raphael says, "My King, your daughter has been in communication with Victoria."

The King says, "I know she has been here for a while trying to find a way to get back in. Listen, my children, she will get to Victoria, but her heart will guide her to make the right decision. Remember, I gave her a gift, and she will be strong through this test."

When I look at my brothers, they all bow and walk away. I don't understand. Why do they just walk away? No arguing! Nothing!

I go home and think about everything that has happened from the time I was summoned up until this night. What are my brothers hiding? Why won't they tell me who this woman is?

As I look at the stars and close my eyes, I think about what the woman said. Where is your strategy? She's right. I must have a strategy. I can't just say "touch of love." All night, I ponder on my strategy, and finally I come up with a strategy that will answer all the questions.

I know that they do not want me to speak to her, but what she is saying does make sense. I have always trusted my brothers and my King, but I cannot help but wonder if they are mistaken somehow. I know they would not lead me astray, and I know that they would never willingly put me in harm's way. They are probably being overprotective. There is not much I can do about that. That is one of the problems with being the baby in the family.

Still, I do not have time to dwell on it. Before anything else, I need to work out an answer to this test. If I don't, any other questions I have, might never be answered!

CHAPTER 5

The sky shines brightly with heavenly stars. They glimmer like glitter scattered across crushed velvet, and twinkle overhead with a calm light. I feel as though they are guiding me, but to what?

I could sit here asking myself that all day. There was no point asking questions though. This was a matter of action.

It's time for the second test. Gabriel walks into the main hall where I am, looks at me, and asks, "What's on your mind?"

"A lot," I say. He has amazing skill for reading me. It is almost as though he can see straight into my spirit being, except I know that he can't, because if he could then he would know exactly what I had overheard. I have so many questions on that, but I can't ask about it. This one, I need to sort out myself.

He smiles at me. "Let me show you something."

As he extends a hand, I am more than happy to follow his guiding sweep through the door.

He takes me to an unknown part of the mansion. I have never seen a door made from the heavenly language, but as I look at it, it is breathtakingly beautiful. I am lost in awe. I can't help but enter a dream like state as my lips part gently. For a while it feels as though it is me and the door. Nothing else.

If my brother had not spoken to me, I could have been lost for hours, maybe forever.

"This door was created by the Elder Son of the King. This door is the way to Life, the way to live mortal life. On the other side of this door are the Rules for Humans written by the Son and King."

He touches the door, and we walk in. The floor is see-through, and the walls are filled with books on how to follow the guidelines of the Son and King.

My brother tells me, "Pick a book."

I reach over him and pick the book, <u>Discernment</u>.

"One thing you need to learn is discernment."

"I already know about discernment, brother."

"No, you don't. Not like this. There are different levels of discernment. The level you will be tested at is the highest level. Let me show you another room. Now, no book can leave this room, so you must put it back, and we'll be back to look it over later."

That seems like a shame. I love to read and to learn, but like he said, there will be time later.

As I put the book back, Gabriel says, "Look."

I look out the window and see Raphael walking with Azrael. I still wonder what Azrael's purpose is in the heavens.

I call over to them, "Raphael!"

As Raphael lifts me up to hug him, Gabriel informs him of the secret room he is showing me.

Raphael says, "Let me take Victoria with us. I want to show her something. Victoria, I know you have been hearing a strange voice and I want to tell you to stay away from her. She's an enemy of the King."

As I look at Azrael, he looks down at me and says, "The female voice you heard was my sister, and she was the most beautiful angel you have ever seen; her hair was as black as the darkness in the sky, her eyes were violet, and her wings were as strong as an ox."

Through all these compliments I can hear a tinge of darkness.

While walking, Azrael stops in front of a wall, and he starts speaking in an ancient language, one that I do not know. The wall disappears, and I can see the vastness of dark space. As we walk into the dark space, I see a book with no name. The only thing I can see is a crown engraved on the front of the hard cover.

Azrael looks at me and says, "Victoria, on your one hundredth birthday next year, find me between the second and third heavens; call my name, and I will come."

I say, "Azrael, why are you telling me this, and, Raphael, why aren't you saying anything?"

Before I can speak any further, Azrael says, "You are asking the wrong question. The question you should be asking is what's in the book. Why must I find you to obtain the information in the book?"

I look at him with confidence and say, "Why? What does this book have to do with me?"

"Victoria, this book contains all the information about every angel, every angel's purpose, and how we are to use the gift provided by the King. The book tells about the war that caused the King to banish his first son from Heaven."

I let out a low whistle. So, few angels must have held this book, let alone read it. This is getting real, almost too real. I look at the book and then back to him. This book must be meant only for top rank officials, and I am to become one of them. It seems crazy but something within me tells me that it is completely sane.

"Wow, that is interesting, but why are you telling me this?"

Azrael walks away and does not respond. Sometimes angels can be frustrating. I know that it is for my own good, but it is so tedious sometimes. I suppose I will have to find them myself.

Raphael says, "Victoria, you still don't get it, do you?"

I say, "Get what?"

Raphael says, "It's not time yet, but when that time comes, you will be—" and before he can finish, the trumpet sounds off a cry for intruders.

Michael appears and touches my head while saying one simple word, "Sleep."

***

I wake up five days later with one thought, what happened?

I hear Gabriel calling my name, "Victoria, it's time to get up."

I get dressed and walk downstairs to see my brother standing there with the book of discernments.

Before he can say anything, I ask him, "How is it possible that I was asleep for five days and what happened while I was sleeping?"

My brother says, "I will explain later after your test. I understand you want to know, but we can't waste any more time."

Who is he to say *I* am wasting time? It was not me that chose to sleep for five days. That was Michael's doing. It was his power that bid me to sleep.

I say, "Why is it always, I will explain later?"

This is starting to feel like déjà vu. All I keep hearing is later, later, later. When I am Queen, I will be able to demand to be told now, but I'm not yet. I am just their sister.

"After today, an order from the King said that we must explain the details of what happened five days ago and why we had to put you to sleep."

I look at my brother and tell him that he better because this is getting out of hand.

"Victoria, there are three levels of discernments: knowledge, understanding, and wisdom. You must get to level three. In the book of Proverbs Chapter 3, verses 13–22, Solomon speaks about all three levels; listen as I read:

Happy [blessed, considered fortunate, to be admired] is the man who finds [skillful and godly] wisdom,

and the man who gains understanding and insight [learning from God's word and life's experiences],

For wisdom's profit is better than the profit of silver,

And her gain is better than fine gold.

She is more precious than rubies;

and nothing you can wish for compares with her [in value].

Long life is in her right hand;

in her left hand are riches and honor.

Her ways are highways of pleasantness and favor,

and all her paths are peace.

She is a tree of life to those who take hold of her,

and happy [blessed, considered fortunate, to be admired] is everyone who holds her tightly.

The LORD by His wisdom has founded the earth;

By His understanding He has established the heavens.

By His knowledge the deeps were broken up, and the clouds drip with dew.

My son let them not escape from your sight,

But keep sound wisdom and discretion,

and they will be life to your soul (your inner self)

and a gracious adornment to your neck (your outer self)."

After Gabriel finishes the passage he is reading, he asks me what I think. This is a difficult question. I have read this verse very many times before, but it is not the kind of thing that someone could understand after one read through. Even then their interpretation may change throughout their lives as they gather more experiences.

"I have a lot to learn," I say.

He laughs, but there is a note of pride in his tone. "Look at me, sister. You must believe in yourself."

Gabriel gives me a minute to think, and after that I ask for some time alone.

Alright, I have two tests that pretty much surround the same thing. The first test is on wisdom and how to use it to defeat the darkness in the world. The second is discernment, but I must get to level three. This is all so interesting. Why are the first two testes centered on wisdom?

Gabriel finds me sitting on a tree stump and asks, "Are you ready for the rest of test two?"

The rest of it? Of course, that wouldn't be all.

"Sure, why not?"

He takes my hand, and we zoom to a quiet little town on Earth with bushes, trees, and a red barn. The barn has three windows, one of which is broken. The front door is old and has three cracks in it. Out comes a young man with legions of demons in him.

Gabriel says, "This is your test, which has two parts. The first part is to tell me which one the stronghold, and the second part is how we would bind the stronghold. Pay close attention to them and watch. It's always the one you least expect it to be. You have one week in Earth time to figure this out. In addition, I want the answer for test one. I will be leaving you here on Earth for one week. You are well protected; they can't even see you."

"I really have to stay?"

"Yes. Michael will be watching you very closely."

As I start to speak, he disappears.

Wow, there are a lot of demons! They creep and crawl, making puppets of men.

How do I figure this out? Okay, Victoria, calm down and watch; pay close attention.

I notice this young man is wealthy. His equilibrium is off when he walks, and I can see that he has mental illness. This is unknown to him, which is very strange. Usually, there is an alert that goes off in a human that the King put in their minds. This is so interesting; the legions have caused a block in this young man's emotions. I'll keep watching. Day one is almost over, and I wonder what my brothers are up to. I must work this out...

Nobody said this would be easy.

CHAPTER 6

This test is taking longer. Much longer.

Before the sun rises on the second day, I see the spirit of addictions, and as I look closely, it radiates to his mate even stronger. I wonder if the stronghold is coming from her—the woman. Being part of the royal family, I have the power to look at a person's life from birth on up. This talent was gifted to me on my adoption but cannot be given outside of the family.

I use this talent to look at this man. When he was born, his birthmark was shaped like a snake. When he was five years old, he was beaten by his mom and sought love from anybody who could provide it. His left eye is weaker than his right eye; he has no friends and is always lonely. He used to date a low-level witch without even knowing. I can see she transferred two spirits into him. One is addiction, but the second one is very well hidden. I wonder why?

The young man's name is Brandon. As I watch him leave for work, he shuts and locks the door. His house is surrounded by darkness. The legions have taken over for the most part, but I can still see an old woman in the house. She has been praying for two days now, asking for immediate deliverance. She knows that he's possessed, but because of her past sins, she's not strong enough to perform the casting out. So many of the people of this kingdom have lost their power. If only they had a little more faith...

See, what humans don't realize is that your past sins can cause you not to move to the next level of power. Like us, humans have a hierarchy of ascension too. Getting all the way to the top gives the grand prize of entering the gates of heaven.

However, her prayers are at least keeping the legions at bay.

While following him to work, I notice that every time he talks to someone, the spirits of anger and sarcasm are at work. The second spirit transferred to him is working, but it is so well hidden, I can't see to call its name. Brandon clocks in, and he starts being mad and sarcastic to each one of his coworkers. He calls them names and purposely sets them up to fail or to get fired. The legions are playing with his thoughts. One of them is always protecting the stronghold. Someone calls him on the phone, and I can tell he has a lying spirit within him as well. The whole conversation on the phone is a lie. He clocks out and goes home. Seeing so much darkness makes me sad, but I cannot dwell on that. I still need to figure out the first and second tasks.

While on the way, the spirit of sadness comes upon him and starts damaging his brain internally. Sadness can take total control of the human brain, but unfortunately humans don't realize that laughter is what heals the sadness.

He makes it home, and the woman who was in prayer all day goes out to the kitchen to prepare dinner for him. The stronghold is still protected, but there is a strong and familiar smell about him. I know it from somewhere, but I can't remember. I must meditate to remember this very familiar smell.

After Brandon finishes his dinner, he takes a shower and goes to bed. The old woman is still praying. She is protecting him, but she is also his hindrance.

As I go into meditation, I recall my two tests and what my brother told me of my abilities.

"There are two worlds; one world is full of darkness and sin, and the other world is full of light and peace. Do you make the decision to keep them separated, or do you slowly introduce more light into the darkness without corrupting the light?"

Gabriel said, "This is your test, which has two parts. The first part is to tell me which one the stronghold is, and the second part is how we should bind the stronghold."

I give a nod and my answer all in the same beat.

"This power makes you stronger, more intelligent, and better able to see weaknesses." This was the power given from the King.

Hmm, what is your weakness, stronghold, and why are you hiding? In my meditation, I recall my brothers in conversation about different types of strongholds, but these were the top three, and I think one of these is possessing this man.

The first ones are spirits of divination. They are used by diviners, enchanters, wizards, witches, charmers, spiritists, magicians, astrologers, sorcerers, necromancers, soothsayers, and false prophets.

The second are unclean spirits that afflict people' minds and souls. They are responsible for unclean thoughts, immoral acts, depression, oppression, and possession. When Marcus controls individuals with unclean spirits, he can also operate in all spheres where those individuals are active.

The third, and last, ones are lethargy spirits, which cause the attitudes of laziness and sluggishness...

He shows signs of one and two, but I believe this stronghold is functioning as a high witch. As I go into deep meditation, I have flashbacks of my brothers in a Heavenly War when I was a little girl. I remember a beautiful angel yelling my name and reaching out to me.

Michael stands in front of me and stretches out his sword saying, "The King rebukes you. Your existence is no longer written in the Book of Creation. You are an outcast. The strength of your wings is dying. You are no longer Queen."

Then I black out. He says her name, but I cannot remember it... I want to remember it, but I cannot. It will not come to me... Why can't I remember?

CHAPTER 7

On days three and four, I follow Brandon around and watch him interacting with people. I also watch the old woman. She does the same thing every night, praying for him. There is still a little time for me. I can keep going. There is a chance that I can still work this out. It may be looking bleak, but I must keep faith in what I am doing. Especially around these demons. There is so much darkness in this place. I must be the light that leads the way.

However, something looks strange about her as she bows her head to pray. Hmm, this may be interesting. I wonder who this old woman is.

There is nothing I can determine. I cannot explain this feeling. I just cannot identify it. I am growing stronger with each day, however, before this would have scared me. Not knowing is terrible. That is why rules and orders help so much. At least now, I am content to stay and work it out.

I step outside on the fifth morning and ponder on everything. I do a search of the house and the old woman. I learn a great deal.

The house is three hundred years old, and before the old woman moved in, no spirits were attached to the house. The old woman moved in, and unclean spirits such as depression followed her. When she got delivered to this house, it never left, but rather attached itself to Brandon. On the third and fourth days, Brandon is extremely lazy and depressed. He starts to get worried, and depression takes over his mind. The spirit of addiction makes it known to him that he's one of the strongholds because he starts to smoke and talk in chanting spells. The spirit is developing like cancer in his lungs.

Gabriel comes down from the heaven and says, "I am ready for test one and two answers. I want details with an exit strategy. Your statement will be recorded in the book of tests! I'm ready."

"Brother Gabriel, for the first test, I will send words of wisdom, knowledge, and understanding through seers and prophets. They will instruct them with the word of the King and the guidelines by which they should live. It will take time, but it will work. In addition, I will work with the King on a more effective strategy. The King's strategies will be more valuable than my plans."

He nods and lets me continue to speak, "For the second test, there are two strongholds. The first is addiction and the second depression. See, the old woman unknowingly brought the depression spirit to his house, and when she got delivered with it, it never left. Thus, it jumped into the body of the man because of his vulnerability from a previous girlfriend. He left himself open for other spirits to enter. The addiction spirit kept depression hidden because it knew that if the depression got cast out, it would weaken addiction. It will also weaken him and force the other spirits to leave. Brandon can be delivered by first removing the old woman from his house and then doing a spiritual cleanse."

There is a long pause in which I feel my chest tense. I am certain I am right, but his hesitation gives me cause to be nervous.

Suddenly, he smiles, and it flows through to me.

Gabriel looks at me and says, "Well done, sister! Know this: the higher the level of tests, the greater the wisdom, knowledge, and understanding is required. Oh, and regarding the second test, your brothers and I handled it. We visited the pastor and informed him of his friend and how to perform the deliverance and cleansing. Victoria, follow me."

We go back to Brandon's house. He looks younger and healthier, and he smells of fresh Heavenly roses.

Brandon is clean. It has always amazed me how human beings allow their environment and body to get infected with the spirits of this world. Why can't they see it? Why are they so blind?

My brother hears my thoughts and tells me, "When you have been around garbage so long, you become that very thing you are surrounded by. Come, it's time to go home."

And just like that, we vanish.

Test three is on its way and I am ready for it. Success is so close that I can taste it, and it is as sweet as honey made by bees in the garden of Eden from the most fragrant nectar of the flowers.

Test three is not long away, and I cannot wait.

CHAPTER 8

We are back at the main gate of Heaven, surrounded by its beauty and holiness. White lines every wall and the light are blinding to anyone who is not blessed. It is a Holy and Sacred place. Its beauty is endless.

After I walk through the gate, I return to my mansion to freshen up and meditate.

It feels good to be home. I slump into my bed which is softer than my feathers. I spend the day relaxing and recuperating my mind. The challenges have been hard on me and I had not realized how much they had taken out of me. I just need a few hours to chill.

Later that night, I meet with my heavenly friends.

Let me introduce you to them. I think you will like them. In fact, I know you will. They are so very wonderful!

Dina holds all knowledge of time. She tells me that knowledge requires much studying, but since she is the holder of knowledge, it is already in her. One time, we snuck into Michael's room and rearranged his weapons. He was very mad.

Next are Enoch and Elijah. They are two funny characters. Enoch watches over all the prophets and the faithful. Elijah watches over the pastors to make sure they are preaching and teaching the word of the King. One day, Elijah took me to a church where the preacher was not teaching the word of the King, and when he recorded it in the book of life, the pastor's life span was shortened.

I have missed them so much, and I'm glad to see them.

I enjoy the time I can spend with my friends while talking about old stories and my new adventure, which is interesting to all my friends.

Recounting old stories is something we all love to do. What is even more lovely is that a lot of these memories include my brothers too.

In fact, once, when we were a little younger, Dina kept turning back time as Raphael read the good book. He read the same story three times with a furrowed brow before he realized that she was using her powers of chronology to turn back his pages. He chased us out of his room after that, telling our other brothers that we were now their problem and that they would be babysitting us from then on.

I depart after a few stories and laughter and go home to rest.

My brother Raphael appears and says, "Victoria, follow me."

"Can I please just have some alone time?" It has been so nice to just be me, to reminisce with friends. We must all make sacrifices, but I need to remember why I am doing this.

"No!"

"Fine! But you don't have to be so demanding about it."

He scrunches his eyes angrily but relaxes by the time we get to the room. He never can stay mad at his baby sister.

As I follow him back to the bridge room, he closes the door and says, "Let the darkness engulf the room. In darkness and emptiness, we stand."

The room turns into an empty, completely dark space.

Raphael says, "I will now tell you about a story that has been hidden from humans and certain angels in the kingdoms."

I nod, letting him speak. Finally, finally I feel like I am getting somewhere.

"Long ago, before the Earth and certain realms of the third Heaven were formed, the King and his four sons, Joshua, Michael, Gabriel, and Marcus, and his daughter, Layla, were a happy family; there was no sin, no disagreement; all were in one accord. They were equal in wisdom, knowledge, and understanding, but each one specialized in one or more unique gifts. Layla was the most beautiful angel, and she could always get her way. The King presented her with a gift, which was a husband on Earth. He blessed her with the ability to have children and to experience a family of her own called humans. She could still access Heaven and use her powers, but she had an issue with the man the King presented her with; he was too equal for her liking.

Marcus was the most charming of them all and nursed the idea to take over for his father, the King, no matter what was required. He loved music and could sing. His singing was rapturous.

Gabriel was the humblest of them. He followed the King's instructions to the letter, and for that the King blessed him with being his messenger. See, that's an important job that no one had except him. He knew secrets that scared even us.

Michael was the fighter among them and was always ready to go to war at any time for the King with no questions asked. The King gifted Michael with strength because of his loyalty.

Joshua was loving and caring. He loved the King and always kept the balance between him and his siblings.

Marcus was and is still jealous of Joshua because the King gave Joshua a little more power and responsibility, according to the King. This was because Joshua never desired power, only love and balance."

I notice that the sin involved here is not disobedience, but jealousy of power and love. One can't even explain the level of frequency and unbalance it causes in the cosmos. The mortals must really try harder to keep that in check. It does no good. It will only damage their soul. They should focus on their own happiness and if they want more, then focus on creating it. Gather more, not try to pull down others. Destroying those makes you jealous will only lead to breaking their life into pieces.

My brother continues.

"The King knew of Marcus's pride and jealousy of Joshua, and he even knew about the betrayal that would soon come. Joshua loved Marcus and always tried to make him happy, but it was never enough.

I say, "Wait! My brothers are the King's children?"

"Yes, but there is more."

Confused, I ask, "What happened to Michael, Gabriel, and Layla during this time of drama?"

"Well, the King sent them off on assignments: Michael and Gabriel were on assignment in the second heaven. Layla was on assignment in the first heaven; hers was the most difficult because of submission. Layla confronted the King and rejected the gift he had given her. She said it made her feel imprisoned.

"Something happened, something unspeakable; Marcus and Layla conspired against the King and their brothers to take over the third heaven. They started with the outer court angels, influencing their thoughts with lies and saying the King was using them for his good and that when he was done, he would kill them. Some of the outer court angels were loyal and didn't believe Marcus. But remember, he's gifted with charm, so his words could poison any ear that was not 100 percent in tune with the King. Layla worked on the inner court angels with her strength of manipulation."

"Goodness..." I hardly knew what to say. This just levelled up so much higher.

"When the war broke out, the King commanded Michael and Gabriel to go from the second Heaven to fight the rebellion in the third heaven. The King banished Marcus from the third Heaven into the second heaven. When the fight in Heaven broke out, Layla was pregnant with you, and the King knew it, so he held her prisoner in the Forbidden Realm, which is one of the darkest and most powerful realms in the Kingdom. He left her there until she gave birth to you.

"Once she gave birth, he thrust her out of the third Heaven into the second Heaven with her brother. The King cursed his daughter by shutting up her womb and taking away her beauty. Layla was the only angel who could have children; that was the King's gift to her when he gave her an earthly husband. The war in Heaven lasted for seven days."

"..."

"So many angels died during the war, and the second Heaven was filled with blood and revenge. I had never seen and felt so much hatred from the fallen angels. After the war was over, it took about two weeks to repair and reorganize the chain of command."

I swallow, remaining silent and listening. How could one person, even an angel, take all of this in?

"Marcus took a good amount of our leadership with him, so we had to move some angels up and moved some back down. The anger was indescribable. For the first time, the second Heaven was filled with fire, blood, dark magic, and a brother and sister covenant was made in a cloud of witnesses to one day take over the first and third heavens."

"..."

"Now do you see why the King is putting you through these tests? We are at war!"

That is when it hits me.

"So, Layla is my mother?"

"Yes, she's your mother. You are the only spirit being here in the third Heaven who has legal access to all three realms beside Joshua. Your mother is trying to turn you against the King, and I think it's time for you to wake up from this mystery voice and stand on the truth that you hold."

Suddenly, we hear a loud boom. We run out of the room, and the angel guarding the front stairs door of the second entrance says, "This has never happened before. The Prince of the Air is trying to get in!"

Raphael says, "Victoria, hide in the throne room! There is a window. You will see it as soon as you walk in toward the right. Stay there, and you can see all that's happening. We call that the Window Above."

How can I process this?

Where do I start?

Me? The daughter of a traitor?

My brothers' sons of the King? Blood!

Am I the only adopted one?

What do I do?

The answer is simple. Run.

CHAPTER 9

As I run to the throne room, I see strange-looking angels and spirit beings I have never met before. There are angels with unique armory, carrying shields and swords with special stones around them that seem to be shining with energy. The spirit beings are as bright as the sunlight. Some have an outer lining of fire around them, and the others have a lining of coldness.

I run into the throne room, and the doors shut. As I look out the window, I can see all three realms; it is beautiful.

I hear my name, softly, "Victoria, Victoria, Victoria."

I turn around from looking out the window. It's the King. I bow down, which is the normal behavior, while not looking up.

He says, "Look at me, Victoria."

I look up, and the King transforms before my eyes. He has white thick hair and is wearing a purple and red royalty robe with a golden crown. His skin is as brown as a wooden table. I cannot see his face because it is as bright as the sun.

He says, "My daughter is trying to break into the kingdom to take over the throne, and her heart is broken because I took what was precious to her."

I reply, "Me!"

He says, "No, Victoria, it was this."

He straightens out his hand and shows me a fruit I have never seen before.

"Bite into the fruit," he commands.

I trust the King, so I do as he says. I reach out and take the fruit from his hand. I bite into it. I feel myself going back to the beginning, and I can see everything rewinding.

The fruit tasted so delicious but what I see is... unnerving...

Never in my wildest dreams did I ever imagine it could be anything like this. It is a lot for me to handle, too much.

But I must handle it, and with them banging on the door, I must wrap my head around it quickly.

Time is ticking away. The hourglass is nearly empty. I don't even know yet what my third test is, and I just found out that my mother was Layla... I carry Layla's blood. Traitor blood.

CHAPTER 10

I see the beauty, the stars, and the emptiness, and I feel the silence.

The King says, "This is how everything began: empty and silent."

"It's so peaceful."

"Yes, this is what I want my children on Earth to experience, the peace, silence, and emptiness, to be emptied with no burdens and to walk with me. Unfortunately, two of my children have had other plans, all because of power. Power can make you mad, and therefore you won't see the beauty in all things. Layla was my beautiful creation. I wept when she rebelled against me. My oldest son was beautiful as well, but I created him with music. My oldest son understands the rhythm and the flow of life. I gave that to him as a gift that he misuses in the Earth realm.

"I know you are wondering why I brought you here."

"Yes, my King."

For the first time, I feel genuinely happy and at peace. I have every right to be mad and upset, but in my heart, I can see why they didn't tell me until I was older. I can see why he was protecting me because I was never of any importance to my mother.

The King says, "I brought you here because it's time for you to know the truth. I know your brother informed you of what he knew, but I will tell you everything from the beginning. You look worried."

"I am because the kingdom is under attack."

"Victoria, I know everything. Your brothers and the Angels of Secrets have everything under control. Everything was planned.

"In the beginning, the darkness and silence engulfed the space. I birthed my children with love, and each one was unique. During that time, we were so happy, and laughter filled the emptiness. We were so joyful. I created other spirit beings, and I allowed my sons and daughter to create some with me. We lived in harmony for the longest time. As time went on, I decided to bless each one of them with a unique gift that they would oversee. Your mother was the most beautiful, smart, and clever spirit. What I loved about her was that she had the gift of words. She could take anything and make it sound so profound. I loved all my children, and I wanted us to be happy forever, but as always there's an imbalance looking for an opportunity to present itself.

"That heavenly day was very unusual. I noticed signs of uneasiness in Layla's eyes. She had just come back from Earth, and she was fussing about the man I created for her and how he wanted to have access to Heaven. She thought that I shouldn't grant him the right to access this realm."

"Well, what is your reason for not giving him access?"

"She stated that he wanted to be part of the family and have power like her."

"What's so wrong with that?"

"She said that he was not like us. She said that he was always saying how she should be doing everything and asking her to help him with the duties. She said that she was Queen of Earth. She also complained that he commanded her to give him some of her power. She made it very clear that she served no man.

"I told your mother that earth was a gift to her and that she is supposed to be able to balance her life as a spirit being and human being. I told her that she needed to experience an earthly life without ruling it but as an equal."

"My King, if you are all-knowing, shouldn't you have known that something like this would have happened? Why would you want something this bad to happen?"

"Let me explain. Yes, I knew this would happen, and even if I wanted to stop it, it had to happen for the entire plan to fall into place." The King clears his throat before continuing:

"I knew exactly what was going to happen. But, as I loved Layla so much, I wanted to make sure she was happy with the gift I had given her even though I knew it would end badly. This was her final test, and she failed it. She didn't understand the importance of what she was given: being Queen and being human. She failed, and she knew it."

"I can understand that."

"She was being tested, and I needed her to pass it. Victoria, even when you know all, it doesn't mean you intervene for a better outcome. I saw what was going on inside her house there on earth. It broke my heart to know and see all these things, especially since I already knew what would happen. Nonetheless, I watched her from the heavenly clouds each day. She made her choice, and she made it known. I saw a huge amount of conflict in their house. They loved one another, yes, but the fighting always got the first prize."

"What were they fighting about?" My mind races with so many questions.

"You see, gender plays a big role on Earth. When I sent Layla down to Earth to begin her own family, we both knew that the fact that she was a woman would influence her life severely. In those days, a woman's place was at home. She had to be submissive to her husband at all times and often endure periods of abuse."

"That's awful!" I say. I am starting to form a better understanding of Layla's situation.

"Layla, having access to Heaven, didn't want to be submissive. She wanted to be the head of the household. In those days, it simply wasn't accepted that a female stood at the head of the house. Her husband didn't see it that way either. He wanted to be her equal and stand beside her at the gates of heaven. Of course, Layla didn't like this one bit, and that is what caused most of their quarrels." The King pauses for a moment.

"Yes?"

"Layla made it very clear that her husband had no right to enter the heavens as he was not worthy enough to be there. Layla didn't want him to be equal to her, but she expected him to bow down to her as she had more power than he, although it was terrible in those times."

"So, Layla denied him access to Heaven?"

"Yes. She didn't want him here and didn't want him to have the amount of power she had. She wanted to be the best and most powerful."

"I see," I say. "It must have been terrible to have that happen and actually know what was going to happen beforehand."

The King looks away from me for just a second. I think I can see a hint of sadness in his eyes.

"Yes, it made me very sad to know this. I let my feelings get in the way of a power much greater than we will ever know. I loved her so much. I couldn't bear to see her changing the course of history. So, I decided to change history on my own accord. I wanted her to come back to Heaven and leave her earthly life behind. I wanted to take back the gift I had given her, just so she could be here with me. I didn't want to banish her into the next Heaven, and I knew that it was exactly what I had to do for history to take its natural course. Instead of letting events happen as it should have, I tried taking away her gift because I knew she wasn't going to pass the test and that she couldn't handle it. It did not work, and that is why we are in this war. Not only was she angry that I had known all along that she would be banished, she was also angry that I tried to take away a gift that I had blessed her with. She could not believe that a father would take away a gift from his own child."

"Love is a powerful thing. You only did what your heart told you to do," I say, trying to put his mind at ease.

"It is powerful. Too powerful! That is why we are here today."

"So why is she trying to get to me? What is her purpose with me?"

"Layla has a very strong and dominant soul. She wants things done her way, and she would do anything to undermine the course of history so that I take her back into this Kingdom. Although I once wanted to do that, I can't. She is not the same person anymore. Her mind is corrupted by evil thoughts of revenge. The love I had for her will always be there, but in her heart is the even stronger power of hate. You see, if she gets you to listen to her and obey her, she can take over your abilities and take your rightful place as Queen. She will then tear the entire kingdom down."

"So, Layla is actually trying to trick me?" I ask with astonishment.

"Yes, she is trying to make you believe and see things that aren't real. I am protecting you from her. Your uncles are out there fighting for you. They love you just as much as I do. At this point, we are fighting hate with love, and although they are both very powerful, only one can prevail."

"The entire kingdom is at war to protect me?"

This broke my heart a little. Somewhere deep down I had always known that I was destined for more. Maybe not a Queen, but more than I was doing. Despite that, I did not want to see people war for me. War means death. I do not want people to die for me. It feels as though I am facing more tasks and challenges than the three, I am set to endure. Speaking of which, there is still another to face. I know it will be the hardest. I am ready.

CHAPTER 11

My mind is racing with the reality of things. I finally understand what all the tests have been about. I understand why my brothers kept so many secrets from me. They wanted to keep my mind and heart pure while completing the tests. They knew that if they told me the truth before I started the tests, it would cloud my judgment. It would steer me in the wrong direction and cause me to fail the tests. And if I failed, Layla would have even more reasons to want to let the kingdom fall to ruins.

It all makes sense now. It is as if something switched on in my head.

It doesn't mean it doesn't hurt though. I finally find my mother; I discover who I am and... It just hurts. I feel as though a little piece of hope in my chest has died. She has killed a portion of me, taken some of my innocence away which will never be replaced.

"I now know the dangers and the wonders of this Kingdom. I know it is my duty to lead those within the Kingdom with love and forgiveness." I tell my King. I have understood balance. I am ready to bring the light, but in doing so I have to absorb a little shadow. I need to understand myself, and those I will be saving.

"You speak like a true Queen," the King says.

I close my eyes and see what the world outside looks like. There is blood everywhere. People and angels are screaming, some covered with flames and others with ice. I see my brothers fighting with all the power inside them. I can see that one of my brothers is hurt and losing his power fast. It breaks my heart to see them fight for me. They are willing to die to protect me from the harm they are facing right now.

Hot tears streak my cheeks and I taste salt in them. The taste is bitter but nothing on what I can see.

How could a mother, *my* mother, do this? Why cause so much hurt? Why?

With the power I have in me, with every single fiber in my soul, I will my power toward my uncles. I will it to seep into their wings, their minds, and their hearts. I push it forward, my own heart aching. I use the pain as fuel. They will win. I must keep telling myself that. Good will never submit to evil. It is as simple as that.

Without speaking, I hear my brother's thoughts.

Thank you, Victoria, for being here with us. Your spirit guides us to finish this war in triumph.

The battle rages on, beautiful lands stained crimson. I feel the point of every blade as if they are cutting me, not my uncles and brothers. With every sparkling tear I weep I thrust that pain forward. With gritted teeth I reach down, stretching into the depths of myself.

I can do this. I can do this! I am the Queen!

A blinding light fills the entire kingdom. The angels are used to being filled with bright light, but this is something I have never seen before. What surprises me even more is that the light is radiating from within me. It flows through every window, every crack, and every darkened corner of the heavens. The war outside comes to a halt as the spirits and angels look around for the source of the light.

As the light starts getting brighter and brighter, music comes with it, like a choir of heavenly angels singing a soft song. A huge explosion fills the kingdom. All the warriors and fighters fall to the floor and cover their eyes. For a few more seconds, the entire kingdom is cast in a fierce light like nothing ever seen before.

There is silence. Pure silence...

As everyone regains their sight and stands up from the dirt, something amazing happens. The light that radiated from me has destroyed all our enemies! All that remains is dust that slowly settles to the heavenly floor.

"And to dust you shall return," the King says.

I drop to my knees, panting but the King lifts me up. He will not have me kneel. Not when I have passed the third and final test. Something even more powerful that I had presented this quest to me, and I have flourished in a flood of white light.

It seeps into the grounds of heaven and heals the very lands and waters. As the men and women drink, they recover.

"What just happened?"

"The truth brought power to you. It brought the power of a Queen to you, and with it you destroyed the enemy."

Gabriel stumbles into the room. "Layla is destroyed! She is gone! Victoria, she is gone!"

He comes over to give me a hug and to thank me for helping them to finally overcome the evil that so nearly destroyed everything.

"Victoria," the King says. "Come here."

I go to stand next to the King as he looks straight into my eyes.

"I know I am making the right choice this time as I am getting older. I give you the gift to be able to determine which spirits take over human bodies. You need to use your gift to find these spirits and destroy them. With your love, forgiveness, and purity of heart, you will guide this kingdom to the future. You will also, as a Queen, be able to make Earth a better place for people to live."

Now, the King, Gabriel, and I stand outside in front of all the angels in heaven. They all bow down to us.

I am Queen Victoria, watcher of the Earth. It is I, Victoria, who will lead you all to a future better than any other.

To be continued...

AUTHOR BIO:

Alicia Robinson currently resides in Baltimore, Maryland. It is her passion for faith and love of writing that inspires and drives her forward. She spends her free time inspiring others and spreading the word of God. Victoria: The Rise of a Queen is her first published novella.

You can find out more about her by following via
Facebook: Bible Talk with Alicia,
Twitter: @BibleTalkAlicia,
and YouTube channel: Bible Talk With Alicia.

Made in the USA
Lexington, KY
13 December 2019

58516211R00051